NOV - - 2013

ANTON AND PIRANHA

D1466690

This edition published 2013 by
Andersen Press Limited
20 Vauxhall Bridge Road
London SW1V 2SA
www.andersenpress.co.uk

1 3 5 7 9 10 8 6 4 2
First published as *Anton Taucht Ab*, 2010, by Beltz & Gelberg

© Beltz & Gelberg, 2010
All rights reserved. No part of this publication may be reproduced,
stored in a retrieval system or transmitted in any form, or by any means,
electronic, mechanical, photocopying, recording or otherwise,
without the prior permission of the publisher.

The right of Milena Baisch to be identified as the author of
this work has been asserted in accordance with the Copyright,
Designs and Patents Act, 1988.

The translation of this work was supported by
a grant from the Goethe-Institut which is funded
by the German Ministry of foreign affairs.

British Library Cataloguing in Publication Data available.

ISBN: 978 184 939 6196

Printed and bound in Great Britain by CPI Group UK Ltd,
Croydon, CR0 4YY

Selwyn Public Library

ANTON AND PIRANHA

By Milena Baisch

Illustrations by Elle Kusche

Translated from the German by Chantal Wright

ANDERSEN PRESS
LONDON

I'm going to tell you a story. It's an adventure story so it has a hero, and that hero is me: Anton of the deep. It begins back in the time when I was known as Starflashman. Here, have some crisps. There's popcorn too. But you have to sit still and listen, all right?

Right. The story begins on the motorway. We had set off. I was already wearing my swimming shorts. Granddad was driving the car and Gran was singing along to the radio.

'Step on it, Gramps!' I said to Granddad. I like a car with some speed under the hood. And I thought how fantastic it would be if all the other cars moved over as soon as they saw us coming.

But Granddad could only do sixty because of the caravan.

The caravan. I looked out of the back window and there it was, wobbling along behind us. If it were a space shuttle, I imagined, then we'd be a team of astronauts on our way to base. I'd be the space captain taking Gran and Granddad safely to the moon. At three hundred thousand miles an hour.

'We'll meet again, don't know where, don't know when . . .' sang Gran. Music from the olden days made my ears queasy. I quickly pulled out my hip-hop CD and passed it forward to her. Then I leaned back and looked out of the window. The left window, that is, because on the right all you could see were cars overtaking us.

The campsite was pretty cool. There were slot machines, there was table tennis, a café where you could buy crisps and ice cream, and there was even a disco. I jumped out of the car, wearing my swimming shorts, you remember. My back was covered with patterns from the car seat because my shorts were the only things I had on. Anyway, I shouted out, 'Venga, amigos!' and ran across the campsite.

It quickly became less cool, because no matter where I looked, there was no swimming pool.

'You're having me on, Granddad,' I said as I stomped over to him.

'Of course I'm not,' he answered. He had towed the caravan over to our pitch and was unhitching it from the car.

'Where on earth is the swimming pool, then?'

Gran laughed. 'We're by a lake.' She said and put her arm round me. I hate it when she does that. I'm not a baby any more! I pushed her arm away and stomped off a few steps. My stomps were quite firm, you know, they might even have caused a bit of an earthquake.

'You cannot be serious!' I started out quietly, but things didn't stay quiet for long when Starflashman was involved. 'You want me to spend my holidays here? *Here?* Hello! What were you thinking?'

Gran and Granddad were quite befuddled. They hadn't counted on the fact that a kid might expect a swimming pool. Sometimes I wonder what planet they're living on.

'But we came especially because of the lake,' Granddad said.

And Gran asked: 'What do you need a swimming pool for as well?'

What a question.

If there had been a swimming pool I could have jumped in headfirst. I would have bombed and held my breath for two to three minutes under water. I would have dived and grabbed the girls' feet, or maybe even their bikini bottoms. I would definitely have saved children from drowning when their armbands sprang a leak. If that had happened I would have swum the entire length of the pool underwater to rescue the small child from the bottom. I'd have brought it to the surface as fast as lightning and handed it to its despairing parents who already feared the worst. I'd have said, 'Oh, by the way, I believe this child is yours.' And I'd have put on my sunglasses and then lay down on the lounge chair. Yes, sir, there were no end of things I could do if there was a swimming pool around.

I didn't exchange a word with the two traitors for the rest of the evening. They unpacked their things and put them in the small cupboards in the caravan. I sat on the sofa watching an action film.

When the film was over, I turned the sofa into my bed and lay down to sleep, right there in that smelly place in the middle of nowhere. I wasn't homesick, or anything, but I did think about the ant game. That's when Mum tickles me as though there are lots of ants crawling all over me, and then Dad picks me up to squash all the ants and afterwards I always fall asleep right away.

But that wasn't an option now. I was one hundred per cent alone. In the holidays. In a place with no swimming pool, where even a rat would have hitched the next ride home.

The next morning something poked me in the stomach and woke me up – a pesky fishing rod. I turned over but then a silly little buoy hit me in the nose. I pretended to sleep and tried to carry on dreaming the lovely dream I'd been having.

I'd been dreaming about a mission in the desert. I was a fighter pilot and my job was to save a village that had been surrounded by lions. I was just about to free a pretty girl from the claws of one of the beasts by hoisting her up into my plane when . . .

'Where have my worms got to?' Granddad muttered – supposedly to himself, but I heard it loud and clear nonetheless. I opened my eyes at once.

'Did you just say *worms?*'

Granddad turned towards me. The fishing rods he was holding in his hand brushed over my face. 'Ah, good morning, Anton,' he said. And then he started looking in the drawers under the sofa that I had turned into my bed. I jumped onto the table.

'They were in a round container—' Granddad mumbled.

But he was interrupted by Gran calling from outside. 'Are you coming to have breakfast?'

Through the caravan window I could see my favourite Crunchy Crisp Chocolate Delight Flakes on the table.

I didn't want to walk through the worm-infested caravan, so I reached for the skylight with both hands. I pushed off the table with my feet and started swinging. I swung forward and back two or three times and then, when my legs were pointing towards the exit, I let go.

The fridge shuddered as I crashed into it. There was an almighty thud. And my little toe, which I had banged against the corner of the fridge, really, really hurt. But I didn't cry.

After breakfast Granddad started messing around with his fishing tackle again. By then he'd found the container of worms and stashed them inside his fishing bag. Gran put on her swimsuit. It looked as though they were going to the lake. That was fine by me. Old people are into one thing and kids are into another. Each to his own. I was planning to leave the sofa as a bed for now. I wanted to watch some TV and maybe have a second helping of Crunchy Crisp Flakes. They were really, really tasty.

I had just got settled in and was zapping through the first few channels when there was a knock on the window. Gran was standing there wearing her sun hat. 'We're off!'

I waved at her cheerily. 'Have fun!'

'Anton, come on!' She knocked on the window, more loudly this time.

And that's when the trouble started.

I had to go with them to the lake. They made me.

I said: 'You can't make me do anything. I'm a free person.' And then they got worked up because

8

I was still in my pyjamas.

I didn't see the problem.

They could have left me in the caravan. They could have left me in my pyjamas. They could have had their peace and quiet. But, no.

So I went with them. I tramped across the campsite behind two old people. One of them was wearing a hat and carrying a sun umbrella. The other one was carrying fishing gear, hitting quite a few people over the head with his fishing rod without noticing. But I didn't say anything. I didn't say a single word all the way there because I was still cross. You can't be cross and talk at the same time.

At least the lake was right behind the campsite. There was a bathing area with sand, and a wooden jetty. Kids were running along it and bombing into the water. Gran and Granddad walked along the shore for a little while until they found a spot they liked right next to the lake and then unpacked all of their stuff.

I stayed near the trees, a few metres away from the shore. Gran walked over to the lake barefoot. She waved her arms about as though she was on a

tightrope because the ground was hurting her feet. When she got to the water, she stuck one foot in.

I got goose pimples.

'Oh, it's lovely!' she called. 'Come on, Anton! Let's go swimming!'

She turned towards me and waved. I didn't move one inch.

Have I already mentioned that I *hate* lakes?

It was gross. I could see them from a distance – the creepers and all the icky stuff along the bottom of the water. Well, to be honest, I couldn't actually *see* them because I was at least ten metres away from the shore. You can't look into the water from that far away. But you *can* see the surface of the water and that was enough. The surface of the water was . . . black. *Ugh!*

It gave me the creeps. Why is lake water black, and why is swimming-pool water such a lovely blue? You get my point.

As black as it was, the lake couldn't have even contained very much water. It had to be full of creepers and filthy yuck. Glibbery fishes shooting

along in all directions and slibbering against people's legs. Mussels opening and closing and pinching people. Snails secreting slime. Fish secrete stuff too. They wee into the water – and who knows what else comes out of them. And that's not to mention the jellyfish!

But the creepers are the worst of all. They come from deep, deep down, from the very bottom. It's even blacker down there, and it's ice-cold. And then they grow upwards, getting slimier and flubberier the further up they come. And when people swim across the surface of the water, their stomachs and legs brush past the creepers.

If I had an enemy, that's where I'd throw him.

Stop laughing! This is serious. You haven't seen the lake. Count yourself lucky! If you don't stop laughing, I won't carry on with the story.

That's better. And now listen carefully, OK?

Gran was in the water. She swam on her back for a little bit, and then on her stomach. She called out: 'Yoo hoo, Anton!' But I couldn't look.

So I put on my sunglasses. There was no need for people to know that I was freaked out at the sight of my own Gran swimming.

Granddad turned to look at me. 'Shall I teach you how to fish?'

'No need.' I straightened my sunglasses on my nose. And then I sat down on a tree trunk that was far away from the water.

Granddad speared a worm on his fishing hook.

That evening there was a bad atmosphere in the caravan. I had fetched crisps and ice cream from the café and was sitting in front of the TV, watching a car chase. But Gran and Granddad wanted us all to play a game.

There they were with the ludo set. I couldn't give them my full attention. Three BMWs were after a Ferrari. One car flew over a bridge, another went under it and it all ended in a massive pile-up. Wicked.

'You really are old enough to play by yourselves,' I said to Gran and Granddad.

But they wouldn't take no for an answer. So when the adverts came on I had to have a serious chat with them. It turned out that they were worried about me.

'Everything's cool,' I said. 'I'm fine.'

'But you didn't go swimming,' Granddad said. 'You were so excited about it on the way here.'

'Do you know how to swim?' Gran asked. 'We can teach you.'

'You can't be serious, Gran.'

I explained to her the difference between being *able* to swim and *wanting* to swim.

'Right then. So you don't *want* to go swimming,' Granddad said. He seemed to have got it.

Gran still wasn't happy. 'But if you don't go swimming, will you enjoy your holiday? Won't you be bored?'

Granddad nodded. 'That's what we're worried about.'

I didn't want a little thing like that to spoil my grandparents' holiday. So I promised not to spend the next few days sitting on a tree trunk for hours at a time with my sunglasses on and a grumpy face. I promised to take some stuff with me to the lake. And I promised to make friends with other children.

'OK?' They didn't seem all that convinced. I held out my hand to Granddad: 'Let's shake on it.'

He shook on it. Then I took Gran's hand and kissed it. And then, finally, they both smiled again.

You see, that's how easy it is to keep your grandparents happy.

And I quickly turned the sound back on because the adverts had just finished.

Granddad was fishing again, Gran was swimming again. I was investigating the lay of the land with my X3C. My Power Racer X3C remote-controlled car was a faithful companion. You could always depend on its three gears and its oversized tyres, even off-road and in puddles. I should know, I had put it together myself.

I'd promised the two oldies that I would keep myself entertained, so I was. And because I'm a good grandson, I was going to keep my second promise as well – to make friends with other children.

It was a ridiculous mission. In my normal, everyday life, I would never have walked around looking for friends. There were heaps of kids on the internet. I had more chat buddies than anybody else I knew. But life stabs you in the back sometimes, and so here I was, in a smelly place in the middle of nowhere, and I had to find some real children.

To make myself less noticeable, I cruised the X3C up and down the beach. Did I already mention that it can go through water? When you gun it with two wheels in the water and the other two on dry sand, it looks pretty good. Water splashes everywhere.

For a while I stood and took in the sorry sight. It was impossible to ignore the fact that there was a lot of bombing going on off the jetty. Man, oh, man! If there's one thing I can't stand, it's children jumping bum first into creepers.

While my hands were manoeuvering the X3C's controls, I kept an eye on what was going on. There were five children on the jetty. Well, not so much *on it* as running across it. They did a run-up, jumped into the water – *splash!* – bobbed up to the surface, swam to shore and stomped across the sand. And then off they ran again, over the jetty,

into the water . . . And so on.

Mental.

One of the boys looked older than the others. He was bombing backwards. Each time he shouted, 'Caramba!' He was definitely a show-off. His hair was shaved at the sides and bleached blond on top. I'd be lying if I said that he didn't look like a show poodle.

A voice next to me suddenly interrupted my thoughts. 'Hello!' I turned round to face it. A girl was standing there. She was out of breath, probably from all that running along the jetty. Her hair was dripping and she smiled at me.

'*Aah!*' I screamed out loud and ran away.

There was a creeper sticking to her shoulder.

I only ran a few steps, of course. Then I stopped before things got embarrassing. Slowly, playing it very cool, I walked back towards the girl. I forced myself not to look at her shoulder.

The girl looked at me in amazement. 'Are you all right?' she asked cautiously.

I didn't answer right away. I didn't want to give

the impression that I had completely flipped out because of a creeper. First of all I fiddled with the remote control and sent the X3C flying. The engine howled and sand and lake water spurted up from under the wheels. The girl watched the performance.

'Hey!' a couple of grown-ups called out. 'What are you playing at?'

They were upset because some dirt had flicked onto their towels. No problem. I steered the X3C towards me. It did whatever I wanted.

'Are you staying at the campsite too?' the girl asked.

I nodded.

The show-off with the poodle hair-do got out of the water. He'd obviously noticed that something was going on and was looking in our direction.

'Did you forget your swimming trunks?' the girl asked.

Now I needed a good answer. Forgetting your swimming trunks isn't cool.

'I can't wear them,' I said. But that didn't sound very cool, either.

'Why not?' the girl asked.

Before I could come up with an answer, Poodle had arrived. 'Is he new?' He pointed at me.

'Yes,' the girl replied. 'But he can't wear his swimming trunks.'

Poodle eyeballed me from head to toe. I eyeballed Poodle. He was a full head taller than me. His shoulders were broader than mine and the muscles in his legs bulged.

While he was staring at my legs, which were pasty and didn't bulge at all, he ran his hands through his terrible hair-do.

Water sprayed into the air.

A few drops landed on my arm. Not only had the drops of water come from the yucky lake, they'd been on Poodle's head as well. I gritted my teeth.

'Why can't he wear them?' He laughed. 'Are they too tight?'

'Don't worry,' I replied, keeping my cool. 'They fit my perfectly honed body just fine.'

In the meantime the rest of the jetty kids had joined us. They stood and looked at me. They were all wearing swimsuits and they were all dripping. As well as my trousers, I was wearing a T-shirt, belt, underwear, socks, sandals, hat and sunglasses too. I knew it was time to say something slick.

'What's your problem?' I raised my eyebrows and looked at the poodle questioningly. 'Halloween's not until October.'

The kid spat on the ground near his feet.

'Nice costume, though.' I smiled a mean smile. 'Ha ha. Next year I'll go as a poodle too.'

Poodle flexed his leg muscles. 'What's *your* problem?' he hissed.

But I wasn't interested in continuing the conversation. I started up the X3C again. Its tyres splashed sand onto the poodle's feet.

He looked down with a stupid expression on his face, and I took advantage of the moment to make my exit.

But as I turned round and walked off Poodle had the final word: 'You haven't seen the last of me, mate!'

I needed to think. Poodle was spoiling for a fight. I could see it in his eyes.

I steered the X3C away. I thought it was better to avoid the bit of shore where Gran and Granddad were lounging. I didn't want them to see me hanging about by myself. So I went in the other direction. There was only one path and it ran all the way around the lake.

There wasn't much to see, really. There were trees, and people going swimming or coming back from swimming. The X3C flew over some tree roots at top speed. A couple of people got annoyed when it drove into their heels by accident. I said sorry, of course. I wasn't trying to hurt anybody.

But I had the right to do whatever I wanted with my X3C. Everybody else was having their fun, after all. They had the lake.

I couldn't fight Poodle. That much was obvious. I was a committed pacifist. So what was I going to do? However I looked at it the only thing I could think of was to hide from him for the rest of the holiday. Even if that meant I was a bit of a loser.

When I had made it halfway round the lake I looked out at the water. At the black soup. There were a few rowing boats on it, and a couple of fishermen were sitting on the shore. And on the other side, directly across from me, was the jetty, still full of children running along it and jumping in. Behind the jetty was the sandy beach where people lay on colourful towels.

I picked up my X3C and thought: *There must be something special about that disgusting old thing. What do people see in it?* I left the path and climbed over branches and leaves, cautiously making my way over to the lake.

I was brave enough to go right up to the water. I was Starflashman, after all, and it wasn't as if I was

afraid of the lake. I was just grossed out, completely grossed out.

Well, there I stood. My toes had nearly touched the sludge soup. I looked down. By the shore, at the very edge, the water wasn't deep at all. Only a centimetre or so. It gradually got deeper the further you looked out.

I was surprised that the shallow water at the edge wasn't black in the least. If you held your head over it and looked down, it was actually completely see-through. The water there was fine. And there was sand underneath it. That wasn't so bad, either.

I thought about how it might feel if I put my toe in. Maybe an electric shock would magically pass from the water into my toe, and from there through my entire body. I would be filled with extraordinary powers and would glow like a laser. Then I'd take off from the shore and fly over the lake. I'd visit the people in the rowing boats. And I'd dive in headfirst, into the middle of the lake, right where it was blackest, to do battle with the creepers. I would destroy every single one of them with my laser arm then I'd drag myself to the beach with what remained of my powers. And the people would cheer, because right there, instead of the festering sludge soup, there'd be water, completely see-through and light blue. Like an extra-clean swimming pool.

A noise interrupted my thoughts. It was a quiet splashing noise. I looked in its direction. A frog was swimming through the water. I looked down at my feet and was happy that I was standing on dry land.

The voices from the beach on the opposite shore rang out. I could easily make out what they were saying. It was a loud 'Caramba!'

next day a proper heat wave arrived. I put on my swimming trunks. They weren't tight at all, so why shouldn't I wear them? They would be a lot more comfortable today.

I went with Granddad to his fishing spot. I planned on spending the day there, for a number of very good reasons. First of all, my eyes needed a rest from poodles and bombing. I pretended I wanted to learn how to fish from Granddad so that he and Gran wouldn't keep worrying. That was Reason Number Two. And third, my grandparents had a cool box. It stood right next to Granddad's fishing chair, all day long, and it was full of ice-cold drinks.

So I took a computer game along and found a nice shady spot.

'You have to spear the bait properly.' Granddad held out a worm. It wriggled in the air and curled up into itself. 'Otherwise they won't swallow the hook.'

I pulled myself together as best I could. I looked at Granddad's worm for a second, then I cast a glance at the cool box. Granddad wanted me to put my own fishing rod into the water, but I persuaded him that it was better for me to watch first.

There's quite a lot to do when you go fishing. You have to set everything up, throw out the fishing line properly, and think about the right kind of bait. And you have to pay careful attention to whether the line is moving. On the other hand, in between doing all of those things, you have a lot of spare time. I played on my computer game and drank nice cool lemonade.

I had just got to a really important level when Granddad suddenly jumped up. A fish had bit on the line and I was supposed to pay careful attention, but by now I was annoyed with the fishing thing.

'First you let out the line. This bit's like a game

27

between you and the fish.' Granddad walked excitedly up and down the shore holding the fishing rod. 'If you don't let out the line, he'll tear himself free.'

I imagined a giant fish down there in the black soup, a shark fighting with Granddad. Granddad had taken off his shirt, his chest was brown and he was wearing a silver chain around his neck. The way he was reeling in the fishing line and talking to the shark was really cool. Sharkbane would be a good computer-game name for Granddad, I thought.

'Come on, laddy, come on. You're not a big one now, are you?'

Then Granddad pulled the line right out of the water. The fish danced and wriggled about on it. Granddad swung it over to me. 'Look at that!' And the fish flew right past my nose.

I shouted: 'Take it away. Take it away from me!'

I got all hot. I think I had a panic attack. Whatever it was, my forehead was covered in sweat. I had to wipe it off.

I could scarcely watch the next bit. Granddad took the fish off the hook while it was wriggling around in his hand. Then he threw it in a bucket made of blue plastic that he had already filled up with lake water.

The fish bucket now stood right between me and the cool box.

By lunch time I was so thirsty that I couldn't bear it any longer. Did I mention that it was a really hot day? And, unlike all those people who were swimming in the lake, I had no way of cooling off.

So I walked in a large circle, all the way around the lake. I even got dangerously close to the edge of the water. That way I could approach the cool box from the other side. I turned my head away from the fish bucket and grabbed a bottle without looking. It was Granddad's home-made iced herbal tea. The next bottle I fished out was of lemonade. I would rather have had orangeade, but never mind. Closing the cool box without looking was difficult. I didn't manage, of course. The lid wouldn't fasten. And that's when it happened. My gaze fell on the bucket with the fish inside.

The fish moved.

When I got back to my shady spot, after circling the lake again, I started to feel a bit better. I held the bottle to my forehead and my neck to cool myself down. Then I picked up my computer game again. But for some reason I kept thinking about the fish.

I had only glanced for a millisecond but I was amazed at what I saw. First of all the fish was nowhere near as big as a shark, it was only about as long as my hand. Secondly, the water in the bucket wasn't black. It was see-through, and because the bucket was blue, the water looked blue too. It really did look like swimming-pool water.

The fish was swimming in its own swimming pool. I, meanwhile, was barely able to survive the heat. I had drunk the lemonade. And my shady spot had turned into a fire pit because the sun had moved across. I was at a hard bit in my game. I dreamed of a swimming pool.

How was the fish getting along in his lovely blue bucket? I decided to risk another quick glance. If I'd survived one look, a second wouldn't kill me. Plus, the bucket was standing in the shade.

I watched the fish. He had stripes on his back
and a red tailfin. I couldn't see his teeth because
his mouth was closed. He must have developed
a technique for moving his side-fins forward and
backwards, because he swam on the spot all the
time instead of crashing to the bottom or sinking.

After I while I lost patience. 'Swim in a circle!' I
whispered to him. If I'd been in a swimming pool,
I wouldn't just have swum on the spot waving my
arms around.

But the fish didn't listen to me. So I prodded
the bucket very carefully with my finger. But
only from the outside, of course. I didn't want to
get anywhere near the water. And, you probably

guessed it, the fish started swimming in a circle.

'Fantastic, mate,' I whispered to the fish. But he went back to swimming on the spot.

I tapped another part of the bucket, and this time the fish swam right towards the tapping noise. I tapped again and again, all around the bucket in a circle. The fish swam in a circle too. And when I changed direction, so did he.

It was really cool!

I stayed with the fish all afternoon so that he didn't feel so lonely. We played Swimming-in-a-Circle together or he swam on the spot and I showed him my computer game.

I was just wondering what it would be like to appear on television with the fish when Granddad came over. 'We're packing up for the day,' he said.

And he reached into the bucket and groped for the fish.

'What are you doing?!' I said in horror.

'He's too small to eat so we'll use him as bait. For tomorrow.'

'And what is that supposed to mean?'

'Well, we'll stick him on a hook and hope that a bigger fish takes a bite.'

I thought my ears might puke. 'Does that . . . ?' I spoke very quietly and seriously. 'Does that mean you want to kill him?'

Granddad laughed. He actually laughed!

'We don't need a machine gun to do it,' he said.

As if the choice of weapon was my biggest problem right now.

'I'll smack him against the ground. He'll be dead right away.'

That's when I crossed my arms. 'Forget it.'

I don't want to claim that I was a particularly good friend of fish. But, as a committed pacifist, I was certainly not a friend of senseless murder.

Granddad sighed. 'All right, then. We'll throw him back into the lake.'

That was a typical Granddad idea. First you sort out a wonderful swimming pool for the fish and then he's supposed to go back into the sludge soup. Just when he'd started to feel at home in his bucket.

'Over my dead body.'

'But, Anton, what do you want me to do?' Granddad asked.

'I don't want you to do anything. Why can't we

just leave everything the way it is?'

'You want to leave the fish here in the bucket?'

I nodded. Why not?

'But I need the bucket. I want to take it with me.'

I asked myself why Granddad had become a fisherman when he was more interested in plastic buckets than in fish.

'What happens if there's a storm tonight? The bucket will fall over and the fish will land on the ground with no water.'

What a terrible thought.

'Is that what you want?' Granddad continued.

I shook my head. Then I lifted up the bucket.

'What is it now?' Granddad said, surprised.

I realised that we could put the bucket under the caravan. That way it would be safe from storms. 'He's coming with us.'

And sure enough when I woke up the next day, the first thing I did was look under the caravan. Nothing had fallen over. The fish was swimming on the spot in his bucket, as calm as calm could be.

'Good morning,' I said.

And Granddad asked: 'Can I kill him now?'

That was when I had my first proper tantrum of the holiday. I can get very angry indeed. It only happens once in a while. But when it does it's as though I have a jet-propelled rocket engine in my stomach.

First I yelled at Granddad: 'Hands off the fish!'

Then I knocked over one of the camping chairs. I might have been a committed pacifist, but violence against *things* didn't count.

I yelled at Gran: 'What do you think you're looking at?'

I think I pushed the table over as well. Gran ran away. Granddad kept saying, 'Calm down. Calm down.'

Everything made me angry, and everything that made me angry was flashing before my eyes: the campsite, the children on the jetty, the lake, this holiday in the middle of nowhere. *Aaahhh!*

Then I crawled under the caravan because I couldn't bear to see their faces any more.

Gran came back. She talked quietly with Granddad, and I could tell that she had phoned

home. Mum had advised her to lock me in the caravan until I'd calmed down. That was typical. I'm always being locked in, just because nobody understands.

I was curious to see how Gran and Granddad would pull it off. Gran went towards the door of the caravan. She bent over and spoke in my direction. 'Anton?'

'Lalalala!' I shouted, so that she couldn't carry on talking. I didn't want to move. It was dark and cool under the caravan. I liked it. And the fish was there too.

Then it was quiet for quite a long time. From where I was I could see Gran and Granddad's feet. They were walking up and down in front of the caravan, putting the table and the chairs back on their legs. Then they had breakfast and read the newspaper. They didn't say much.

When all of that was done Granddad came up to the caravan. He said: 'The fish needs new water.'

I pulled the bucket over to me and looked inside. There was plenty of water.

'He's used up the oxygen in there,' Granddad continued. 'If he doesn't get fresh water, he'll die.'

I thought about it. It could be a trap. I could come out. Then they would almost certainly grab me and lock me in the caravan. Or I could just send out the fish. But then they might kill him.

If I stayed down here with him and it was true that he needed fresh water then I was playing with his life. I looked into the bucket. The fish really did look a bit on the wobbly side.

'It's all right, mate. We're in this together,' I whispered to him. He waved his red tailfin.

Granddad's feet were still in front of the caravan because he was waiting for an answer. 'No lake water!' I cried.

Gran had brought a giant jar of gherkins on holiday with her. We'd had gherkins every day so far, and there were at least twenty of the things still to eat. We took them all out. Gran speared them with a fork and I held out plates and cups to catch them.

By the time the gherkin jar was empty, we'd filled two plates and five cups with gherkins. Gran shook her head and murmured: 'Oh dear, oh dear.'

I punched Gran in the arm. In a friendly way. And I said: 'I owe you one.'

Then I took the large gherkin jar and filled it with tap water. Once again Granddad groped for the fish in the bucket. I gritted my teeth. As he lifted the fish out of the bucket with his bare hands, it wriggled around in the air in a really yucky way. But once the fish had arrived in the gherkin jar, he was his old self again. Red Tailfin, my brother.

'It's a perch,' Granddad said. 'He eats worms, insects and smaller fish. He's still very small. But later on he'll turn into a beautiful predator fish.'

A predator fish!

I had seen a film about piranhas once. They're man-eating fish that bite swimmers in the feet. And if you happen to find yourself in the middle of a school of piranhas, *sayonara*!

I pictured my little fish turning into a piranha. Then he could lie in wait in the lake until Poodle turned up doing his show-off bombing. Ha!

I tapped on the gherkin jar with my finger. The fish turned towards me. 'Listen, Fish,' I said. 'I'm going to give you a name. Are you ready?'

The fish waved his tailfin. I sounded a fanfare: 'Ta-da. Your name is . . .'

And I took a deep breath to make my voice loud and deep.

'PIRANHA!'

The gherkin jar was better than the bucket because Piranha could look out. I carried it into the caravan. Piranha looked at the bed, which had been turned back into a sofa, the kitchen, the area where my grandparents were sleeping, and the television. I showed him the car too, but I thought it was better if I left out the fishing gear.

I would have liked to show him the entire campsite, but my arms were going numb. A gherkin jar full of water isn't an easy thing to carry around. Luckily I remembered my X3C.

It was strong enough to transport a gherkin jar. And because I had put it together myself, I knew exactly how to adapt it. I rearranged the parts so that there was a flat bit in the middle, which I carefully placed the gherkin jar on. It still wasn't stable enough. But with Granddad's braces and the rubber bits from Gran's curlers, I managed to fix it in place. Then I drove it backwards and forward a little bit. Piranha seemed to think everything was OK. So I grabbed the remote control.

It was cool! I could drive Piranha around now.

We circled the outside table. The jar wobbled when the car went over a tree root. But it didn't fall over and after that I was more careful.

Gran and Granddad came to find me when they had got ready to go to the lake. 'What are you doing?' they called.

I explained it to them. They wanted me to come to the lake. I didn't think the lake would be particularly exciting for Piranha because that and the bucket were the only two things he'd seen in his life up to now. But I gave in.

So we marched across the campsite. Granddad with his dangling fishing rod, Gran with her sun hat, Anton with a fish in his car.

People stared.

Some of them even spoke to Gran and Granddad. Gran pointed to me and said: 'It was his idea.' She shrugged her shoulders as though she was trying to apologise.

People laughed. I paid no attention.

We soon got bored at the lake. And no wonder, because we'd spent all of yesterday there as well. I sweated and Piranha swam on the spot.

Boring.

'*Hasta la vista.*' I waved at Gran and Granddad and set off with Piranha to investigate the lay of the land. First I wanted to show him everything on the campsite. Piranha would enjoy that because the paths around the campsite were tarmacked so the ride wouldn't be as bumpy.

To get to the campsite, I had to go past the jetty. I didn't like that idea, because the other children had turned up; I could hear them shouting. If Poodle saw Piranha, things could get sticky.

So I had to steer Piranha through the bushes to avoid going past the jetty, there was no other choice. That was when things really got juddery. The X3C dragged branches along with it and sometimes leaves fell into the gherkin jar. I fished them out again quickly and tried to keep Piranha calm.

'I'm Starflashman,' I explained to Piranha. 'That's my computer-game name. That's what my chat buddies call me, but you can call me that too if you like.'

Right in the middle of the bushes, when I had no idea where the stupid campsite even was any more, I heard a scream.

'*Aaagh!*'

I turned round and discovered the girl from yesterday with the dripping wet hair. 'Get lost!' she shouted. Her hair wasn't dripping wet today, but her trousers were around her ankles and she was crouching over the ground.

Hang on to your hard hats, ladies and gentlemen. She was having a wee!

I turned away quickly. It was a bit of a shock because I'd never seen a girl having a wee before.

43

I wanted to sneak off in the other direction very quietly. But there was a twig stuck between the wheels of the X3C. I fiddled with it, getting nervous.

'What's that?' the girl asked. She'd finished her wee, had pulled her trousers back up and was pointing to the gherkin jar.

'That's Piranha,' I replied. What else was I supposed to say? It was too late to hide him, because the gherkin jar was see-through, and the water too.

'That's never a piranha.'

'I didn't say: "That's *a* piranha". I said: "That's Piranha".'

The girl looked at me, then at Piranha and then back at me. Then she said: 'Right'.

By then she had got me so worked up that I jammed the twig even further between the wheel and the axel.

'Is it a boy or a girl?'

'The fish?' I couldn't take much more of this. 'The fish is a fish. A man, a boy.'

'But his name ends in "a". That's a typical girl's name.'

What a clever clogs. 'So what's your name, then? Smarty Pants-*a*?'

The girl laughed. 'No! Einstein-*a*!'

Now I laughed too. 'Or Know-It-All-*a*?'

She sat down next to me on the ground. Slowly she rolled the X3C back two centimetres. The twig rolled along with it. The girl snapped off the front of the twig and then pulled both parts out.

'My name's Marie,' she said.

'Marie?!'

I shook my head. Marie doesn't end in an 'a' now, does it?

Marie explained to me that she never weed in the lake. I hadn't asked her, but she told me anyway.

'The other children all do,' she said.

I was horrified. 'Why do you go swimming in a giant loo?'

She shrugged her shoulders. 'Because it's fun.'

'But weeing in it isn't fun?'

She nodded.

I fired up all my brain cells, but I still couldn't

45

make sense of it.

'If had to choose, then I'd rather wee in it than jump in it.'

Marie stood up. 'I'm going back to the beach. Don't you want to come? Your swimming shorts do fit, after all.' She pointed to them. I didn't like the idea of strange girls thinking about whether my swimming shorts fit me or not.

I shook my head. 'I've got stuff to do.' And it was true.

Marie walked towards the jetty. I went deeper into the bushes.

I got scratches from all the branches. But at some point I found my way out and saw that I was almost at the campsite.

Now I could take Piranha for a walk in peace. I showed him the shower building, the table-tennis table, the little shop and the café.

When I got to the café I realised I wanted an ice cream. But I didn't have any money. It was about time Grandad gave me enough money for a King Royale, the biggest ice cream on the poster. My mouth watered at the very thought. Then I heard a *splash*.

Piranha had waved his tailfin. I leaned over to look at him. 'What's the matter, Piranha? Fancy an ice cream too?' And then cold terror took hold of my bones. I almost fell over. 'Piranha!' I screamed. 'Oh, no, Piranha!'

I started up the car with the remote control and sprinted off that very second. I hated myself. How could I have forgotten to give Piranha something to eat?! He hadn't had a single crumb since we had teamed up. I wasn't his friend, I wasn't his brother, I was a swine.

We fought our way back through the bushes. There were branches in the way again, but this time we went faster. Piranha was very brave. He swam on the spot the whole time, even though the jar did a lot of dangerous wobbling.

As soon as we got to Granddad's fishing spot, I shouted out: 'Money! I need money right away!'

Granddad waved his arms about and said, '*Shhhhh!*' He didn't want me to scare away the fish.

So I whispered: 'Please, give me some money!'

'Are you buying ice cream again, Anton?' Granddad asked.

'Piranha's hungry. He needs something to eat right now.'

'And what are you going to feed him?'

'Fish food, of course!'

I wanted to buy a tin of fish food. I'd seen it on TV once. Somebody who owned an aquarium had had some. There are colourful flakes in the tin. They look like Crunchy Crisp Flakes except they're shaped like crisps. You throw them into the water and the fish bite pieces off.

'But I've got fish food here,' Granddad said. He leaned over to his fishing box. He brought out a plastic container. I could tell what was coming next.

'Never!' I yelled. 'No worms for Piranha!'

But Granddad shook his head. 'We've got something much better than that.'

MAGGOTS.

Maggots are tiny, white things that scurry about and wiggle like worms. Granddad reached into the container, took one out and threw it into the gherkin jar. It all happened so fast that there was nothing I could do.

The maggot disappeared inside Piranha at about the same speed. 'He likes it!' Granddad cried.

I felt ill.

'Can't we give him something else?'

'What?' Granddad laughed. 'Apples? Or biscuits?' Suddenly he looked serious. 'Piranha is a predator fish, Anton. He needs meat.'

The maggots reminded me more of custard than of lamb chops. Granddad explained that they would actually grow up into flies. Well, the ones that hadn't been eaten by fish, anyway.

I began to understand that live maggots and flies were just the thing for a predator fish. A predator needs something to sink its teeth into. So I asked Granddad to give Piranha some more maggots. But Granddad said that he was my fish and I should feed him myself.

I needed a plan, because I couldn't possibly stick my fingers into the tub of maggots.

I looked for a long stick to serve as a crane. And I used a piece of tree bark as a shovel. I fastened it tightly to the end of the stick using some of Granddad's fishing line.

The tool was difficult to use so I sat down between the trees and carefully stuck the tree-bark shovel into the teeming white container, which was standing open next to Piranha's jar.

'Funny taste in food you've got,' I said to Piranha. I managed to lift the bark back out. There were a few maggots on it, but a lot of them slid off again. A few more of them slipped off as I moved the spade over to the gherkin jar.

Bleugh!

But a few did find their way to Piranha. I did the whole thing all over again, because a proper predator needed more than a few crumbs for dinner.

That's when Poodle showed up. I could see his dyed hair shining on the path.

I ducked down quickly but it was too late. He'd spotted me and was coming right over to our

fishing spot.

'Granddad!' I said. I wanted to warn him.

But Poodle had already shouted: 'Hello there!'

Granddad placed his rod in its holder and stood up. 'A visitor. How nice.' He held out his hand to Poodle. 'So you've found some friends, after all, Anton.'

Poodle shook Granddad's hand. Yuck.

'I'm Anton, Anton's Granddad,' Granddad said, being friendly.

Poodle laughed. 'Anton and Anton, ha ha ha.'

I didn't see what was so funny. If I'd been called Granddad, then it would have been a different matter.

'What are you fishing for?' Poodle asked.

Granddad said something about roach and bream and other stupid fish. Who would have guessed that Poodle was a bigger crawler than a tarantula playing hopscotch?

When the two of them were finished with their bla bla bla, Granddad went back to his fishing. Poodle came up to me, puffed out his chest and grinned.

'You started something,' he said to me in the

kind of voice you usually use to say 'coochy coochy coo' to babies.

I stood up slowly. I brushed the dirt off my legs slowly. And in a deep voice I said, just as slowly, 'If I were you I would hide. The RSPCA are on their way. They're looking for runaway poodles.'

Unfortunately Poodle didn't react to my slick line at all. What a waste. He was rummaging around in the gherkin jar.

'Hands off!' Things were about to get serious. I pushed out my lower jaw and rumpled my brow.

'It's enormous!' Poodle cried, referring to Piranha. 'You could get two whole fish fingers out of that!'

I lifted up my maggot-delivery device-thingy and shoved the bark, which still had some maggots clinging to it, right under his nose. He didn't even blink.

His gaze fell on the maggot container. He calmly picked it up, swung it back and tipped it upside down. The maggots sailed through the air and into the bushes.

Then Poodle laughed.

'Buzz off!' I hissed at him. 'Dissolve into thin air! Become immaterial matter! Find a black hole to disappear into! Do something to make the world a more beautiful place and get out of my sight . . .'

'Will you shut your trap?' Poodle groaned, sounding like a grumpy mum with a headache.

Unfortunately I couldn't. Slick lines are my speciality.

Poodle bobbed and weaved like a boxer.

Boxing was not my speciality.

'Come on, then! What about a little fight?' Now he was shadow-boxing.

But I couldn't fight him. I was a committed pacifist. And not just since yesterday. One day, when I was five years old, I had sworn an oath. And I had kept my word ever since. No fists, no pushing, nothing.

Then Poodle pushed me. It happened really quickly.

I looked over at Granddad who was standing on the shore with his fishing rod. He was too far away to hear what we were saying. I wished he was a little closer, over here, next to me.

What was I supposed to do with stupid Poodle? Find another slick line? 'It's no wonder your hair stands on end. If I were your hair, I'd try and run away too.'

Poodle's face didn't react. He pushed me again, harder this time.

'HEY!' I screamed. I tottered and fell to the ground. But the 'Hey' had been very loud, loud enough for Granddad to hear.

Poodle stopped prancing around because Granddad had put down his fishing rod. 'Coward!' Poodle hissed. 'Crying to Grandpa, are we?'

This bit of the story isn't much fun, I agree.

Granddad came over to us. 'Are you fighting?'

I stood up and brushed off my trousers. 'It's all right.' Then I pointed to Poodle. 'He's just about to leave.'

'Oh,' said Granddad.

Poodle said nothing and left.

I was happy to see the back of him. It put me in a really good mood. And I shouted out: 'The RSPCA are coming!'

Granddad didn't understand. But I grinned.

Poodle turned round when he heard that.

He moved his lips and silently mouthed a rude word.

Even though I didn't hear it, I recognised the word. I'd rather not repeat it.

I sat down in front of Piranha's jar. 'Were you afraid, Piranha? There's no need to be afraid of him. He's only pretending. He's not that strong, really. He's probably as strong as . . .' I wondered how strong Poodle could be. As strong as an ox? As strong as a dog? Definitely not as strong as an Evil Critter.

I've got a computer game where you have to fight Evil Critters. They've got eight arms, can run as fast as a horse and bite like a dog. As a player, all you have is your agent's belt. But I always start out by saving five princesses. That gives you a chestful of energy and spirit. Then I finish off the Evil Critters. I use laser tests to find out which of

the robots aren't really robots but Evil Critters in disguise. And I tear the stolen diamonds out of their filthy hands. Ha! 'Now you know why they call me Starflashman,' I explained to Piranha.

Granddad interrupted us. 'Where are the maggots?' He was standing in front of me, fishing rod in hand.

He'd put me on the spot. 'The maggots ran away.'

Granddad stared at me with wide-open eyes. I corrected myself: 'They crawled away.'

'They can't crawl away. They only crawl around in the container.'

'I'll buy you some new ones,' I suggested. I had a bit of pocket money in the caravan.

'There's no fishing shop here.' Granddad looked upset.

And then he said in a stern voice: 'If you lost my maggots, you'll have to get me some worms.'

'But . . .' That was really mean. First Poodle had picked on me and now Granddad. 'It wasn't me.' Let Poodle get hold of some stupid worms.

'Was it that boy?' Granddad asked. 'Did he take our maggots?' Suddenly he sat next to me on the ground and grabbed my arm. 'Was he picking on you?' Granddad was all wound up. 'You have to fight back! You can't take everything lying down.'

I pulled my arm out of Granddad's hands. 'Nah, it's all right.'

'It's not all right. I'm going to talk to that boy's parents.'

'What?'

'Of course I am. They should pay for our maggots. And that boy should say sorry to you.'

'Don't!' I cried. I couldn't imagine anything more embarrassing than that. Was this really happening to me, Anton Starflashman? Good grief!

'Granddad, you'll do no such thing.' I explained it to him very calmly. 'That boy wasn't picking on me. He wouldn't even be *able* to pick on me. We were messing around. All right? We were just messing around. We played for a bit. And that's how the maggots got knocked over. By mistake.'

'I see,' Grandad snorted. He looked like a baby who has had his dummy taken away. I was happy he believed the story. But I felt sorry for him too.

'Come on,' I said, and stood up. 'Let's go and look for worms.'

~

You put a pole in the ground and wiggle it around. That's how you loosen up the earth and then the things come out.

'There's one here!' I called. The worm was wiggling like mad. It had a couple of shiny red patches and it made itself thin and then thick and it was really yucky.

'Grab it!' Granddad cried.

Eeugh!

It was revolting. Granddad came over to have a look. I quickly used my feet to cover up the worm with some earth. 'He got away,' I said.

Granddad found a lot of them. He put them in the maggot container.

'What's that boy called, anyway?' he asked.

'Which boy?'

'You know, the one who was here before.'

'The boy who was here before?'

Granddad paused with a thin worm in his hand. 'Who else?'

I thought about it. Poodle, Poodle. What was Poodle's real name?

'He's called Po.' I couldn't be bothered to think up a nice name for that idiot.

'Po?' Granddad asked. Then he shrugged his shoulders.

'Well, it's nice that you've found a friend.'

He nudged me. Like a proper pal would in a cool film. I suspect he's picked that up from me.

'Cheers, mate,' I said. And Granddad was pleased.

Another worm turned up, a really fat one this time. Covering the things with earth while Granddad put one after another into his container was getting boring. I took a thin branch and used the end to tickle the worm. It wrapped itself around the branch in a really disgusting way. I held the whole thing up in the air.

'That's a nice fat one.' Granddad nodded admiringly. There was no denying that I'd done quite a good job of picking up the worm.

'We can give that one to Piranha.' Granddad pointed to the gherkin jar.

He was right. The best worm for the best fish.

The worm fell into the jar with a loud splash.

'Tuck in, mate!' I called out to Piranha. He

didn't waste a second.

'Did you meet Po at the lake?'

'Of course.'

Granddad was even happier.

'Po's really good at jumping off the jetty. And Marie too.'

'You met somebody called Marie as well?' Granddad was beaming.

'Marie was the first one to talk to me.' It was a lot of fun making Granddad beam.

I kept on talking. 'Marie thinks my swimming shorts are cool.'

'Oo la la!' said Granddad. He whistled through his teeth and laughed. I laughed too. We couldn't stop.

It was great.

When we got back to the caravan that evening, Gran was waiting for us. She'd been shopping and brought us presents. She was very pleased with herself. Granddad got a book with crossword puzzles.

'Do you think I get bored while I'm fishing?' he asked and pretended he was angry about the present. 'You probably think I don't catch any fish.'

'No, no!' Gran cried out quickly. Granddad kissed her to show he was only teasing.

Then I got my present. Diving goggles.

There was some sort of clever scheme behind Gran's present but I couldn't figure it out.

'I thought you might like some diving goggles. You'll definitely enjoy swimming in the lake if you have goggles', she explained.'

Hello?! Why should I enjoy swimming in the lake with goggles? When you wear goggles, you can see EVERYTHING!

I said: 'Thanks.'

Granddad said: 'Your friends'll think that's great.'

'Friends?!' Gran asked.

Granddad patted my head proudly. 'Po, Marie . . . Anton's met half the campsite.'

I gave a tortured grin and nodded.

Gran's eyes opened wide. She was really excited. 'Were you in the lake with the other children?'

What was I supposed to say? So I said nothing. Since I was already nodding and giving tortured grins, I carried on like that.

'Really?' Gran planted a kiss on my cheek. Who cares, let the two of them think that's what I'd been up to. They were always so nice to me, I could be nice back for once.

And so I told them about the swimming beach. 'We don't swim much; mostly we jump in from the jetty.' And I told them about bombing, and that you could shout out, *Caramba!* And I told them about Marie's dripping hair and I told them that I could bomb further than Poodle.

'That's blooming marvellous.' Gran shook her head.

She was still shaking her head when she went inside the caravan shortly afterwards to cook. She sang a lot of songs from the olden days while she was cooking. I was pretty sure I'd made her happy.

But my gaze fell on Piranha and I was ashamed. Piranha had listened to all of it and he knew that I had been lying. I had to make things right.

'**P**iranha,' I said. 'My friend.' That was a good way to start a conversation between friends. I had driven Piranha a short distance in his car. We were behind the shower building where we could talk in peace.

'Believe me, I'm not a liar.' Piranha swam on the spot and listened.

'I did it for Gran and Granddad. They want a good grandson. That's perfectly understandable.

Normally grandsons are cool and jump off jetties. Not me. I'm a loser.'

Piranha batted his tailfin.

'It's OK, Piranha. I can live with it.' And I told him how annoyed everybody would be when I became a space-shuttle pilot. All those people who thought I was a loser.

Piranha swam up and down a little bit.

I thought of Dad. 'It's not nice when your kid's a prodigy but you treat him like a loser,' I explained to Piranha. Admittedly, I was exaggerating a bit when I said prodigy. I'm not exactly a prodigy, but I am a good kid. Somewhere between very good and good, let's say.

I wanted to teach Piranha to say: 'Anton, you'll never learn!' The way Dad always says it. I said it so Piranha could see. You have to make the word 'never' really loud and really long.

'Nev-er!'

My mouth was right next to the gherkin jar and I made the word as loud and as long as I could.

'*Neeeeeeevvvvvvverrrrrrrrrrrrrrrrrr!*'

Piranha jumped. He thought it was stupid, and he was right.

I laughed, but then I remembered the lake again. What a terrible mess. I was a liar and a loser.

No! No, I wasn't, it was the lake's fault!

As I thought about the lake my stomach turned into a jet-propelled rocket again. This time it didn't want to take off into the sky, it wanted to plummet downwards. Straight into the ground.

'Piranha?' I said. And my voice sounded weird. 'Shall we burn down the jetty? We could pour petrol over it and then light it with a match.'

When I heard myself say that, I started to cry.

'Don't look,' I said to Piranha. I was crying like a sad old loser and I was embarrassed.

But Piranha was a friend. He looked the other way.

Shall I carry on with the story? You've gone all quiet. Are you bored? Don't worry, there's an action sequence coming up . . .

Well, the holiday continued. For a few days nothing special happened. Every morning we changed Piranha's water and he got a worm to eat. Gran and Granddad had fun by the lake and Piranha and I wandered about.

The last day of the holiday began exactly the same way. I went to the lake with my grandparents. I took the goggles with me, the way I always did so that they'd think I was going diving.

When we got to the shore, Gran said: 'Run

along! You don't have to waste your time with us oldies.'

'And say hi to Po!' Granddad called.

We had no choice but to leave them, I could see that. The first thing I did was steer Piranha's car towards a certain swimming beach with a certain jetty. I waved goodbye to Gran and Granddad. They both waved back.

As soon as I was out of their sight, I steered Piranha in a different direction. Every metre closer to the jetty brought us dangerously close to Poodle. And he wanted to make mincemeat out of us, as you all know.

So we trotted along at a safe distance and wandered all over the campsite. I couldn't think of anything else for us to look at. Half-heartedly, I steered Piranha over the tarmacked paths.

We walked past the tents and the caravans, but they were almost all shut up. The people were probably on day trips. You could hear the engine on Piranha's car as well. The clock at the reception showed twelve o'clock. I had no idea what I was going to do for the rest of the day.

The goggles were a nuisance. At first I held them

in my hand, but that meant I couldn't steer any more. Then I put them on my head. Not over my eyes. On my forehead. But that meant gave me a headache and the elastic bits pressed down on my ears. I was cross that yet again I had to carry the goggles around with me for hours and hours and all for nothing.

So I went into the shower building – you could hear the flush of the toilets in there all over the campsite. I put the plug in one of the sinks and filled it up with water. 'A mini-swimming pool,' I said. And then: 'Ha ha.' Because thinking about swimming pools wasn't funny at all.

I took a deep breath and dived in. There was no treasure or sunken ships or other mysterious things of the kind that divers normally discover. There were no fish, either.

But what are friends for? I surfaced and took a deep breath. What *were* friends for?! Carefully I lifted up Piranha's jar and slowly poured it out.

'Hang on tight!' I called to Piranha. Piranha slipped out into the sink along with the water. At first he was surprised and swam around in a circle. Then he made big movements with his fins. He shot through the sink from left to right.

'It's fun, isn't it?' I asked.

Piranha zoomed from right to left. He was obviously having fun.

I took a deep breath. And then I stuck my head in and went diving with Piranha. It was like watching a film in 3D!

My head hardly moved at all. I only surfaced when I needed air. And then I submerged again. I held my head in the middle of the sink and watched Piranha.

He was flitting around like crazy. Sometimes he came up to my goggles and bumped against them. The first time it happened I was scared. But I knew there was nothing to be afraid of. It was probably just a fishy way of saying hello. The way people nudge their friends sometimes.

I said to Piranha: 'Hello.' Underwater it sounded like, '*Uuoowww.*' But Piranha came right over and nudged me again. He understood.

I had just put my head back under the water when something rolled over my feet. It was so weird that

I couldn't do anything for a few seconds. I couldn't move, I couldn't think, I couldn't breathe.

After that I did everything all at once and got water in my throat. I pulled my head out of the sink with a snort but I couldn't see anything because my goggles were wet, and because I was too busy coughing. It took me a little while to catch my breath.

'Hello,' I heard somebody say.

I wanted to take off the goggles. But when I pulled at them, my skin went along too – they were stuck to my face! After a few attempts I tried tilting my head backwards and pulling the goggles forward at the same time. It worked.

And then I recognised the person standing in front of me. Who else could it be? Po, the Poodle.

He looked at me the way cool people look at nerdy people in films. And he said with a miniscule smile: 'All right?'

He was holding my remote control in his hand. So it was the X3C that had rolled over my feet.

'Nice to see you again, Poodle,' I said.

Instead of answering, Poodle sent my X3C racing through the shower building. First he backed it up to the wall. Then he made it go full pelt. The car jetted past us. Without steering or braking, Poodle sent it crashing into the opposite wall. My lovely X3C.

'How fast?' he asked.

'Thirty,' I said. Actually it could only manage fifteen, but why tell Poodle the truth?

'Crappy old thing,' he said and threw the control into one of the sinks.

My answer was: 'See ya.'

But unfortunately Poodle wasn't about to leave. He grinned at me. He wanted to give me a hard time. 'Do you think these showers belong to *you*? Do you think this campsite belongs to *you*?'

I hated him.

'Do you think these goggles belong to *you*?' He threw them over to the X3C in the corner. And he came closer and closer. Even without the stupid haircut he was at least a head taller than I was. And I could see big muscles on his arms.

'Buzz off.' My eyes blazed as I looked at him.

But I was a committed pacifist!

Suddenly I was afraid.

'**W**hat's that?'

Poodle was pointing to Piranha in the sink.

I had no idea how to explain to a poodle what I'd been doing. I didn't really *want* to explain it, either.

'Hmm, what could it be?' I decided to win myself some time. 'Maybe it's an elephant. Yes, I think it's an underwater elephant.'

'Shut it. That's the fish from the other day.'

'Shouldn't you be going? The campsite people are bound to throw you out. Poodles aren't allowed in the showers.'

Poodle was still staring at Piranha. Piranha was swimming on the spot and staring at Poodle.

74

'Why don't you kill it?' Poodle asked.

'What did you say? All I can hear is "woof, woof".'

'Did you catch it? It's tiny. Couldn't you pull anything bigger out of the water?'

'If I were you I would stop yapping. You'll give yourself away . . .'

'Stop talking!' Poodle looked at me, irritated. Then he swiped at the water with his hand. 'I'll kill it.'

'No!!!'

I was at the sink in a flash. Luckily Piranha had managed to escape. Poodle swiped for the fish again, this time with both hands. But Piranha was fast.

I pushed myself in between Poodle and the sink.

'Hello, hello!' Poodle said, laughing. 'Are you in love with it? With a fish?' He was starting to overdo it with the laughter. 'That's it! And that's why you stuck your head in there. So you could be closer to it and give it a snog. Ha ha ha!'

My ears felt pukey. 'I'll shut your gob for you,' I hissed through clenched teeth.

Poodle didn't waste any time. He grabbed my

T-shirt with both hands and lifted me up into the air. I hung there with my feet just off the ground.

Then I remembered.

The images flew through my head really quickly. A picture of our kitchen at home. There I am. I'm five years old. I'm playing with my hot chocolate. There's a submarine swimming in it. The submarine is Mum's lipstick. Mum is shouting. She's angry, really angry. She grabs my T-shirt. She shakes me. It hurts, in my stomach, in my ears. My feet are dangling in the air. 'Let me go!' I scream. 'Let me go!'

Poodle didn't let go.

The day with the lipstick in the chocolate was the day I became a pacifist. I didn't want to be the kind of person who would shake somebody. Or hit them or kick them. I never wanted to make another person cry.

That was what went through my head at that moment. And I thought that in all those years since then I hadn't once got into a fight.

And then I kicked Poodle in the shin.

Wha-am!

He let go. He was in such pain that he took three

76

steps back. I could have got away. But I stayed where I was and looked at him.

I couldn't believe it.

'Right.' Poodle staggered to his feet. He was out of breath. 'Now I'm going to pull the plug on your little friend.'

I jumped up immediately and charged at Poodle. But he stuck out his foot and I charged right into that instead. Next thing I knew, I was lying on the tiles.

And Poodle was right in front of Piranha's sink. And before I knew it he had Piranha's plug in his hand.

He waved it in front of my nose. I heard a *glug-glug* coming from the sink.

'Piranha!' I cried. But my voice sounded lost. I had lost. The only thing I could think was, *Please, please, please!*

The *glug-glug* in my ears sounded like a loud, roaring waterfall. And something loud and roaring was whooshing through my body. It was the jet-propelled rocket. The countdown was running.

Ten, nine, eight . . . The countdown bubbled up in me, faster and faster. Three, two, one – ZERO!

It was the best uppercut ever.

I can't remember what my fist did. But it must have hit its mark because after that we were lying on the floor. Both of us. Poodle was underneath me. I pressed his arms to the tiles with my hands. He kicked his legs. I tried to keep him still. For a brief moment I succeeded, and that was when I heard that terrible *glug-glug*.

'Give me the plug, you vile beast!' I shouted down into his face.

He spat at me.

He was holding the plug in his right hand. I tried to open his fist but that was difficult, and I had to let go for a moment to wipe off the spit. Pah!

That's when he managed to struggle free. He jumped up and began to run. As I followed him, my gaze fell on the sink. A puddle! Piranha lay in a tiny puddle that was getting smaller and smaller. He was thrashing his tailfin and it was making a clapping sound. I turned on the tap so that he at least had a shower.

Poodle was getting away. I stormed after him,

out over the campsite. I caught up with him, threw myself on him and hung onto his legs. We both crashed to the ground again.

We were lying in front of a camping table that belonged to some strange people who were playing cards, but I didn't care. Now we were in a proper fight. Hitting, kicking – all that energy was coming from the enormous force of my rocket.

My mind and my body were concentrating on one thing only: I wanted to get the plug out of Poodle's fist. It was incredibly difficult because, after all, he had quite big muscles. I only managed by pushing his body to the ground with my right knee, stopping his arm from moving with my left knee, holding down his left hand with my right hand and tearing at his poodle hair with my teeth. Only then could I separate the fingers of his fist with my left hand and grab the plug.

Gotcha!

'**H**ang on in there!' I cried as I ran into the shower room.

Piranha was shaking all over. His long fish body collapsed to one side and then to the other. The shower was keeping him wet but that wasn't enough water for a fish. His tailfin kept on making that clapping sound.

I was about to put the plug in when I noticed that Piranha was lying directly over the plughole, which made sense, because that's where most of the remaining water was. I couldn't put the plug in without pushing Piranha to one side. He clapped with his glibbery fin and wriggled.

A friend is a friend, and this couldn't be any

worse than Poodle's spit.

I pushed Piranha to one side. I touched him. He was glibbery.

Very glibbery indeed.

As the sink filled up with water, Piranha immediately started to swim again. I was happy because he was happy.

'Everything's all right, mate,' I said.

My gaze swept through the showers. It was chaos! My X3C had lost a tyre. It was leaning at an angle against the wall in the corner, my diving goggles nearby. There were drops of blood on the floor.

Drops of blood? I ran to one of the mirrors over the sink. Hang onto your hard hats, ladies and gentlemen! There was blood on my head. A line ran down my face past my eye and down to my cheek. It had dried in already. I looked a bit of a mess.

If this were a film, then right about now a pretty woman would turn up and put some ointment on my wound. It'd burn like hell.

But Piranha and I were on our own. It was the men's shower room. And I'd been in a fight. Me,

the committed pacifist! What had gone wrong with the world? Hadn't I sworn against violence?

I turned on a tap to get my fingers wet and wipe off the blood. And then my gaze fell on something.

There was a plug next to the sink. I looked left and right. There was a plug next to *every* sink. I realised that I could have used any one of those for Piranha's sink. I also could have filled up the gherkin jar with water again instead of running after that idiotic Poodle . . .

Slowly I looked back up into the mirror. There he was, the kid who hadn't thought of any of those things. His face was all battered.

'I defended you with my own blood,' I said to Piranha. I was proud. I had fought against the big kid to defend the weak. A little fish versus a poodle with large muscles – what could be more unfair? I'd had no choice but to intervene.

On the other hand there was the matter of my oath. It didn't work any more. I was five when I'd taken it. I hadn't known much about the world. Now things were different. Now it was time for a new oath.

'Piranha,' I said and held up two fingers. 'I swear that I will abolish violence. Violence against kids and weak people and fish. But I won't abolish violence against strong people and really stupid people when a friend needs defending!'

To seal the oath, I scratched some blood off my cheek. Then I dipped the bloody fingers in Piranha's water.

Piranha doubled back to me. And when I saw him swimming I was really happy that he was glibbery. Otherwise he wouldn't have shone in the water like a piece of gold.

Back at the caravan Gran cleaned up my wounds. She had a wound spray for kids and it didn't hurt at all. My grandparents complained about the jetty because they thought I had hurt myself while I was swimming. I didn't say anything. But I was happy to hear them say bad things about the jetty.

We spent the rest of the day packing. And there were gherkins for dinner because we still had so many left.

'I hope Piranha won't get bored on the journey,'

I said. I realised that Piranha had never sat in a proper car. He would probably have preferred a boat.

'What do you mean?' Granddad asked.

'I mean, say if we get stuck in traffic again,' I explained. 'Then I can show him my games. He's already seen some of them.'

'Anton,' Gran said, but then she stopped. I looked at her.

Why had they stopped talking?

Granddad was looking at Gran too. She still didn't speak.

Then Granddad said: 'We can't.'

They didn't want Piranha to come with us under any circumstances.

I threw a tantrum.

A proper temper tantrum.

Nothing helped. That was that, game over. The end was near. The end of a true friendship.

That night Piranha was allowed to sleep with me. I turned the sofa into a bed and put the jar next to me.

At first I thought about how I could smuggle Piranha home. In a Coke can, for instance. That way he would have made it back with me. But what would have happened then? Sooner or later I would have been found out. When I went to school, if not before. And I didn't want my friend to spend the rest of his life in a can. So I decided that before we left the next day I had to pour Piranha into the lake. I had promised Gran and Granddad, after all.

After that I didn't sleep much because we only had a few hours left together.

There was a full moon. Light shone in through the caravan window, and when Piranha moved the water by beating his fins, sometimes it shimmered.

The next morning the alarm rang at six o'clock. I had set it so I would be the first one up. My grandparents were still asleep and had no idea what I had planned.

Very quietly I ate a large bowl of Crunchy Crisp Flakes. Then I picked up Piranha in his gherkin jar, and my goggles. I didn't want to throw Piranha into any old corner of the lake, my plan was to watch him swim away and say goodbye to him underwater. Piranha understood me when I talked underwater. I wanted to watch him, but under no circumstances was I going to get into the lake.

That's why I had the idea about the stupid jetty.

I carried Piranha over there. He couldn't ride on the X3C any more because it was missing a wheel, so by the time we arrived my arms were quite sore.

At six thirty in the morning there wasn't a soul in sight on the jetty. We were all alone. So far so good.

The lake was calm. Calm and dark. For the first time I climbed up onto the jetty.

Right at the front, at the farthest end, I put Piranha down. He swam up to the edge of the jar excitedly and looked out. Did he recognise his lake? Was he looking forward to seeing his family again?

Then I lay on my stomach. I slid forward so that my head stuck out over the jetty and hung in the air. There it was, the water, right there underneath me in its full horror.

This was the plan: I wanted to go underwater wearing my goggles. But only the goggles bit, and maybe a bit of forehead and nose. The rest of my body would stay on the jetty and in the air.

I put on the diving goggles. And I bent over. *Aaagh . . .*

It was much too far away. Somehow I had thought that the jetty and the lake were much closer together. I had to slide forward. Now everything above my belly button was in the air. I could feel my stomach muscles squeezing together so I wouldn't lose my balance. It was a great feeling to have stomach muscles.

I carefully stuck my face in the water, goggles first, closing my eyes as I did so. The ends of my hair got wet and I had to hang on to the jetty. It wasn't very comfortable but there was no other way, so I decided to get it over with quickly.

'Piranha, you're going on a journey.'

Just to be able to hold the jar with one hand, I had to lift up my chest and use an awful lot of stomach muscles.

I wanted to tell Piranha: 'Don't be afraid of the creepers,' but that took too much effort. The jar weighed a ton!

Before I poured it out, I wanted to put my head underwater. Otherwise I would miss everything.

But to do that I had to take my other hand off the jetty. It all got a bit much for my stomach muscles.

My legs lost their hold, my stomach muscles gave up, then the heavy jar pulled my arms down and my legs up.

I fell.

I fell into the abyss.

And I landed in the lake with a splash. The lake was all around me and I was all the way in.

It was wet and cold. But I felt hot. A voice in my head was shouting: 'Get out, get out, get out!' My legs thrashed around as I fought my way to the surface using all my strength. My head popped up. I gasped for breath and opened my eyes, but then I got dragged down again. The jar was so heavy!

I could see Piranha swimming in the gherkin jar. I could see him really well through the goggles, which was strange because we were now in the middle of the nightmarish black soup.

Piranha bumped into the side of the jar. He wanted to get out. *I* wanted to get out! But it was Piranha's turn first. I turned the jar upside down for him.

He beat his fins and his body slid into the lake. When he realised that he wasn't in the jar any more, he beat his fins even harder and shot off like

a rocket through the water. He zoomed away with three beats of his fins. The water glistened. The sun's rays had turned into moving shiny patches. I watched my friend disappear into the shimmer. It was lovely and very sad.

'Bye, Piranha!'

It sounded like, '*Buypiwaw*a.'

I surfaced and put the jar on the jetty. It was colder outside than it was in the water. Almost chilly. So I decided to dive under again, just for a moment. Just to have a quick look and see whether Piranha had come into contact with a creeper or not.

It looked good. To be honest, I couldn't even see any creepers. There was something unreal about this underwater world. It was loud and quiet all at the same time.

Then something moved. A tiny dot came up to me. It was a fish. It was Piranha! He nudged my goggles and then swam away again.

'All right, mate!' I called after him. 'Keep your tailfin up!'

I'd swallowed some water because of all the shouting I'd done. I surfaced, hung on to the jetty and coughed like mad as I thought about the shimmers. Piranha wouldn't have such a bad life down there. In actual fact, the sun up here wasn't as nice as it was down there.

I was leaving today. The holidays were over. But I wanted to be close to Piranha for a little while longer. After all, he had been my companion for nearly a week.

So I took off all my wet clothes apart from my underpants and slapped them next to the jar. Then I let go of the jetty again, took a deep breath and sank underwater. My weight pulled me down into the lake.

The water flowed all around me. Whenever I turned round, the water moved. It made little waves that washed up against me. I felt light, but the water felt light too. It was friendly.

Things like water can't really be *friendly*. But that's what it felt like. I swam and kicked my feet with all my might, shooting forward. *Yippee!*

Piranha's swimming style was different to mine. He wiggled all his fins really quickly. I tried to copy

it. My hands were side fins and my legs were the tailfin. Swimming like that meant I had to surface quickly to get air. I hadn't got very far, probably because I didn't have any dorsal fins.

I could really see a lot through the goggles. It was like those underwater films on TV. I hadn't discovered a sunken pirate ship or a submarine yet, but that didn't mean there weren't any. I kept diving.

And there they were: the creepers. Further out in the lake there were great big bushes of them. I changed direction. There were giant stones next to the creepers. They looked great, like cliffs. In fact, they reminded me of some underwater caves I'd seen in an action film once. I pretended I was wearing a diving suit with lots of belts on it and secret-agent's gadgets attached to them. Baddies might be lurking in those caves. Or an Evil Critter! I swam and kicked my feet again and slid through the water without making a sound, just like Piranha. Mine would be a surprise attack. Halfway there I surfaced for air, but I was getting closer and closer to the stones. What if the Evil Critter had an oxygen tank? He might be lying in wait. But I wasn't afraid – I didn't need an oxygen tank. I knew all about camouflage tricks from my secret-agent training so I found the entrance to the cave quickly. Maybe he was inside? There, in the dark hole between two rocks. I'd slide in there smoothly, like an octopus. And surprise him. And discover a chest of stolen diamonds. Brilliant!

Again and again I swam up to the surface where the sun was blinding. I squinted and took in some air. And then I went back down again.

This is Piranha's world, I said to myself. *My friend's world.*

I saw a school of fish. They had black stripes and red fins. Piranha wasn't with them. I would have recognised him immediately. Maybe they were his brothers? Or his sisters? I dived down to them but they swam off straight away.

On and on it went. I can't list all of the things that were under the water. There was so much to see! As I swam and looked about I thought: *I'm underwater. I'm Anton of the deep.*

It was great fun secretly following fish. They didn't notice me because I swam after them without making a sound.

As I was concentrating on following a mini-fish, the kind you can lose sight of very quickly, something touched me from behind. I went hot and cold with fright. An octopus? A shark? A creeper?

Carefully I turned round. And I recognised a small person in a bikini. It was a girl!

I surfaced and took off my goggles.

'Hello!' gasped Marie.

Behind her there was nothing but water. I looked in every direction and all I could see was water. The trees on the shore were a long way off.

'We're right in the middle of the lake!' I cried.

Marie nodded. She was quite out of breath.

'You're not allowed to swim out this far,' I said.

'Oh, so you are but I'm not?' Marie was cross. 'I only swam out here because of you. Everybody's looking for you. On land and in the water. Your gran thinks you've drowned!'

'Drowned?' As I thought it over, I forgot to tread water for a moment and went under a little bit. I quickly started treading water again. This wouldn't be a good time to drown!

'She found your clothes on the jetty.'

'My wet things?'

'Your dry things.'

'They're dry already? What time is it?'

'Don't know.' Marie found swimming on the spot difficult. 'Nine thirty or ten o'clock, something like that.'

I hadn't even noticed how late it had got! We were supposed to leave at ten. 'I'll come with you now,' I said and began to swim the crawl.

Marie complained because I was splashing too much. She was doing breast stroke. Somehow she was quicker than me. So I did breast stroke too.

When I saw Gran and Granddad on the shore, I waved and shouted out: 'Everything's OK. I'm coming!'

They waved back.

We really did have a long way to swim. And it was hard work. But all I thought about was how quickly I wanted to get there. Hopefully my grandparents hadn't already called the police. Hopefully all the excitement hadn't worn them out. After all, they were quite old.

Gran was standing on the sandy beach. She unfolded a large towel and held it up in the air as I dragged myself onto land with my last bit of strength. I fell into the large, soft towel and collapsed into Gran's arms.

'Anton! What happened?' Gran cried.

'Where were you?' Granddad asked.

'Everything's fine,' I reassured them. 'Piranha is fine. I took him home.'

'Were you in the water all that time?' Granddad asked, amazed.

I nodded.

'But we were standing here looking and looking and we never saw you once!'

'That's because he was underwater all the time,' Marie explained. 'He came up for air but he didn't look around.'

That must have been why. And that's why I hadn't noticed how far out I was. 'Like a submarine,' I said.

Marie laughed.

'Marie is good at spotting submarines,' I added. Marie was pleased. I was a little embarrassed.

'Thank you for fetching him, Marie.' Granddad shook her hand. Gran too. So I thought, *Oh well*, and I shook her hand too and said, 'Thank you, Marie.'

Gran rubbed me dry. 'Now, come along,' she said. 'It's time to go home. Mum and Dad are waiting already.'

I peeled the goggles off my head and held the towel like a cloak. I pushed my feet into my sandals without fastening them.

'Are you coming back next summer?' I asked Marie.

She nodded. 'We always come to this campsite.'

'And are we coming back next summer?' I asked Gran.

Gran laughed. 'If you like.'

'Well, that's all sorted then. See you soon,' I said to Marie. And to Gran and Granddad I said: '*Vamos!*'

Off we trotted over the beach. Granddad was carrying the empty jar. Gran was carrying my clothes. I was the last in line, looking like superman in my towel. I thought about my online-chat buddies. Would they believe the story I had to tell?

And then I thought about the ant game. I couldn't remember the last time I'd played it with Mum and Dad. It must have been a long time ago. It's a really good game. It'd be nice to play it again.

What's up with you? You're so quiet and you've been listening so carefully. I'm not used to that. It's a real adventure story with a proper hero, isn't it?

I had to tell you. You had to hear the story of how your son became Anton of the deep.

No, stop! Stop tickling me. You haven't heard the end yet! The end is the best bit.

Stop! Hands behind your back! Otherwise I can't think.

So I was on the beach walking behind Gran and Granddad. I glanced at the lake one last time. The black horror. The sludge soup. Piranha's home.

We walked past the jetty. The horrible jetty. I stopped walking because I had to look at it properly one last time. There was something about the jetty that wouldn't let me keep going.

And then it started, slowly. Deep down in my stomach. The jet-propelled rocket. It was burning, the fire getting bigger and bigger. It was bubbling up inside me.

I turned back to Granddad and Gran. They were still walking. I was going home with them! I was in a hurry! But the countdown had started. Eight, seven, six . . .

Anton, I said to myself, *keep your cool*. Five, four, three . . . The force was too strong. Two, one. ZERO!

And I ran.

As my steps thundered over the wooden jetty,

I threw away the towel. As I ran I dropped my goggles as well and kicked the sandals off my feet.

It felt great to run over the jetty. It was like a launch pad. I ran faster and faster.

And when there was no more jetty, the rocket lifted off.

The air around me moved . . .

'CARAMBA!'

Thanks to
Nicolai, Leon and Ivo.
Carola, Svea, Anja, Ursula.
And Stefanie!
And especially to Hansi.
And to Milena for typing it all up.

Love,
Anton

Milena Baisch studied at the Film Academy in Berlin. In addition to writing screenplays for movies and TV, she has written many books for children. *Anton and Piranha* was first published in Germany where it won the German Children's Literature Prize.

Elle Kusche works as an illustrator and graphic designer. Soon she will finish her studies to become a doctor.

If you enjoyed *Anton and Piranha*
you might also enjoy these other books
published by Andersen Press . . .

WILL GALLOWS
& THE SNAKE-BELLIED TROLL

DEREK KEILTY

ILLUSTRATED BY JONNY DUDDLE

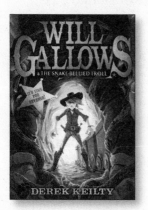

Will Gallows, a young elfling sky cowboy, is riding out on a dangerous quest. His mission? To bring Noose Wormworx, the evil snake-bellied troll bandit, to justice. Noose is wanted for the murder of Will's pa, and Will won't stop until he's got revenge!

ISBN: 978 1 849 39236 5

Read them all!

A Dog Called GRK

By Josh Lacey

What would you do if you found a dog in the street? Would you return him to his owners? Even if they were a thousand miles away – and in prison? Tim finds a stray dog on the way home from school, but his parents refuse to let it into their house. He knows what he has to do. He sneaks out of the house in the middle of the night with the dog, and catches a taxi to the airport, then a plane to Eastern Europe . . .

He will have to break into a high-security prison, pilot a helicopter, and make a nail-biting run for the border in his high-octane adventure with a dog called Grk.

ISBN: 978 1 842 70384 7

Read
them all!

Aunt Severe
and the Toy Thieves

Illustrated by Nick Maland

Daniel gets more than he bargained for when he visits his Great-Aunt Emily one day. She's grumpy and extremely severe because her fiancé, the Colonel, has vanished. Into thin air. And it looks as though two evil toy thieves were responsible.

Soon Daniel is in hot pursuit. But he's not alone. Along for the ride are his aunt, two clumsy ostriches, three even clumsier monkeys and a penguin who never stops talking. Not to mention a very, very sad pink crocodile . . .

ISBN: 978 1 849 39541 0

Also available: